AIR BNB

TERRIKA BELL

SYNOPSIS:

A young newlywed couple embark on their new beginnings. The groom decides to move them out of the country to Japan shortly after they wed. The new bride isn't happy about the uncharted territory and the fact that their new home isn't ready for them to move in. Being more fluent in Japanese she joins him without pause. What would you do?

THANK YOU!!:

God, thank you for my life, my health, my sanity, and keeping me close to you. At times I have not thanked you enough and I apologize. Another project and all I can think about is this is the best therapy I have ever known. You are The Author of my life and I enjoy being the lead character. We make a great team!!! I don't have anything to ask of you.

Simply, thank you!

To Bell & my churn:

You have watched me at my lowest, highest, and in between and never changed up or flinched. I am a hand full and mystery at times but every time I am all yours. I appreciate you all for staying by my side when I am easiest to love but more importantly when I am hardest to love and yet you do anyway! No judgement. I am proud of each of you. Let's continue to "do this", make memories and laugh at the pictures as proof!! I love yall!

To my family/friends/supporters:

Thank you for your support! So many of you have been with me from the beginning. I noticed. If there is anything I can share with you, go for it! Time is not going to wait for you to decide. Time is going to do what it always does and that is continue with or without you. Each day spend an hour or more working on your goals, dreams, and aspirations. Perfect your skill(s). You would rather be ready than to try to get ready when "your door" opens!!!   I'm grateful for each of you.

WEEK 1
CHAPTER 1

FIRST NIGHT

In his heavy British accent Travis calls out to his newly wed Claudine: "Babe are you ready? The car is here for us. It's now or never or as you'd put it "get here now!" He laughs and begins to go looking for her to see what is keeping her. "I…I" Claudine attempts to respond but bittersweet memories keep her lips sealed and her heart full. Travis whispers as he walks closer to her "Awww, dear. I know it is hard to walk away from what we began here. Just think of all the new memories we are going to create when we get there. Somewhere new to the both of us." He stands behind her embracing her with his arms. She closes her eyes. Taking a final deep breath she exhales and a tear drops. The tear drops onto Travis' hand. He squeezes her tighter. She smiled with tears in her eyes and commences to let go of the life they had for the one they are walking into. Fear of the unknown is what kept her stagnant.

The doorbell rang. Their driver was getting impatient as he knew they had to stay on schedule or else they'd miss their flight. An air of melancholy surrounded her. Claudine says: "Let's go. Our new lives are waiting for us. I can stay and catch up with you you know?" Eager to leave and not trying to entertain another disagreement Travis says "Hun, we have already crossed this bridge. Your things are already in route with mine, and as your husband I'd be moved to extend my date to accommodate your decision."

He kissed her on her forehead and whispered: "To new beginnings."

They have arrived in Nago, Okinawa. Having arrived at night the newlywed's felt as if they were on their honeymoon. The view was breathtaking. The night sky above was fuchsia mixed with purple in color. The weather was that of a summer night with a low breeze. The gate to the property was opened awaiting their arrival. The lights from inside the home bounced off unto the in-ground pool. The house looked as if it were made of gold. One palm tree was planted standing in the middle of the patio. The outdoor furniture was luxurious. With there being no blinds covering any of the windows you could see into the home. They were in a hurry to take a tour. "I will get our things and bring them in. Go, take a look around." The driver said to them. Travis hurried out of his side of the car to get to Claudine's side to open her door. The big smiles said they were happy to start their new lives. All of the fear and second guessing she did went out the old window and a new hope looked in to their new windows. The 15-room one-story home 6 of which are bedrooms was an Air BNB owned by the company. Travis signed a two-year contractual agreement that included him relocating to Japan. Their new home wasn't move-in ready. Claudine was hesitant to accompany him as she wanted more time to say goodbye to family and friends. Her fluently speaking Japanese gave Travis more reason to win her over as they discussed reasons why she should have traveled with him rather than waiting until their home was complete. She understood more during their travels especially when she'd catch him trying to speak and translate. She stepped in and saved him every time.

The two of them were like children slowly walking through the home eyes and mouths wide open. They couldn't believe their luck. Travis felt complete. He had been an intern at his company for a year. During a merger the President visited his site because he wanted to meet the young man who wasn't yet employed by him yet went above and beyond to save the company money, give great advice, and were able to keep some of the most prominent people on the team. Travis earned his position, his salary, and all the perks to come. He was patient with the process and showed up despite not being compensated for any of it. He was dedicated to the cause, to the process. For that he was rewarded in an abundance.

Through the patio door they entered the living room. There was an office space behind the couch. On the other side of the glass doors in the living room was one of the master bedrooms. The two ventured into it. Claudine was amazed at the space and layout of this home. Travis was right behind her. He felt more accomplished as her husband than he did the day he said, "I do." The gleam in her eyes and smile on her face was his confirmation of a job well done. Once they walked out of the master bedroom, they glanced over to the dining room with a six-seater table with matching décor from the living room. Cherry oak was on the floor just under the kitchen table, several cabinets, and doors. They walked through and played with the lights and water fixtures in each bathroom as they hadn't seen anything like them back home. The driver had already begun bringing in their belongings but the two were so stuck on touring the home and engaging in their reality they hadn't noticed. Once he was finished, he simply began to converse with the General Director of the company who stopped by to make sure Travis and Claudine arrived safely, give them their keys, and Travis' itinerary. Though his job duties wouldn't begin just yet he still had a few weeks of training that were required. He hadn't decided to complete them remotely or at the office. He wanted to make sure Claudine was settled in had she chosen to join him.

Clearing his throat, the driver wanted to make his and the GD's presence known. Travis and Claudine were sharing a warm kiss and walking backwards towards the kitchen where they started the tour. Neither of them knew the two men had joined them inside the house and were waiting on them. "My apologies gentlemen." Travis said and wiped Claudine's lipstick off his lips. Claudine helped him to clear off the rest. He whispered looking at her: "Thanks, babe." She whispered back: "You're welcome." Both smiling from ear to ear. The GD said with a huge smile: "I guess it's safe to say the two of you made it safely and are pleased with the home and Travis you are good with the company's expectations?" Travis smiled and extended his hand to the

GD because the GD was holding papers for Travis. With a big smile Travis replied: "Yes, sir. More than pleased. My wife (he nodded his head toward the GD), Claudine is happy so I'm very pleased. This is (he waved it to the GD) the itinerary I assume? I will look and any questions I will submit via instant message as instructed." The GD said: "Nice to meet you Claudine and responded to Travis. Then it's all set. I appreciate you making such a bold decision and trusting the process. The CEO promised you many perks, you ain't seen nothing yet. We (The GD looked at the driver) will let you two get settled and enjoy your first night. He turned to Travis, shook his hand, and said: "I'll be in touch." He shook Claudine's hand as well. The driver said: "Have an amazing night. My contact information is in with the other papers he has given you. I am your driver while you are staying here. Once your home is ready you will have another driver. If there is anything you need, I can get or assist you with, please don't hesitate to contact me." He smiled, waited for confirmation, shook their hands and proceeded to walk away with the GD. As soon as the GD and driver go to the back doors the GD turned and said: "I almost forgot." He reached inside his blazer jacket pocket and grabbed a pouch with keys in it. "Travis, these are for you all. They are color coordinated. On the paperwork the colors will explain which keys are for which doors etc. Again, if you need anything or have any questions don't hesitate to contact me. Oh, if you choose to drive yourself around there are company cars to choose from. Let me know. "I, we really appreciate it all." Travis said. Claudine said with a huge smile: "Thank you so much. Really." Both the GD and driver said at the same time: "You are welcome." They headed out of the patio doors and closed them behind them. Travis now had the remote to the gate so when the coast was clear, and he saw that the two men were gone he closed the gates to the backyard. Claudine's eyes filled with tears. Tears of joy. The two of them stood in the middle of the kitchen and hugged one another. His dreams had come true. There were no more goals to cross off his list. He was now to create new memories and continue to live his life to the fullest. His hard work had begun to pay off. "I am glad you didn't let up about me joining you. I love you, Travis. Thank you for being all mine." "I am glad too Claude. You're welcome. Thank you for being all mine."

They kissed and enjoyed their first night in

Japan.

CHAPTER 2

CHOICES

Travis walks up behind Claudine and puts

his arms around her embracing her. "We've

broken in the place (he kisses her on her

neck) let's say we get out for some fresh air. I don't have to check in with my colleagues for a while. Let's go sightseeing." He waits for her response. Claudine grabs her cellphone from her pocket and stares at it. She changed the settings on her cellphone so she could keep up with the weather, time zone change, and news in Japan and back home. "Babe, it's Thursday and 1:50pm here but back home it's already Friday and 2:50am there. Wow, this will take some time getting used to. If we are going to be living like this, I can get used to it though. Yes, let's sight see. She agreed." "Which bathroom do you want to use this time for our showers?" Travis asked. "Ion know babe. The fact that we get to choose from a few is still blowing my mind. I mean I just don't know. Do you want to soak in a Jacuzzi tub or shower in one of the wall-mounted shower thingies? Everything in this house is brushed with gold. I love it here." Claudine said. Neither of them could decide which bathroom to use. "Let's add a little fun to making our decision. I say let's write down the choices and with our eyes closed we each choose which bathroom to use." Travis said. Giggling: "Ok. Let the fun choosing begin." Claudine said. Travis grabbed a piece of paper and began writing out the bathroom colors. Each bathroom had a different color theme in it, so he began to name them on the sheet of paper according to their color scheme. Claudine was anxious to play so she decided to help him write out the bathroom colors so they could hurry and choose. Once they finished writing all the colors down on the piece of paper Claudine said: "On the count of three we both will choose. Hold up. If our eyes are closed how we know where we are pointing? Claudine asked. They both laughed. "Good point." Travis said. "Hmmm. Let's use our ink pens to point to the color. If it lands on a specific color that's where we are going and if not, where it lands closest to that's the color bathroom we will choose." 'Ok." Claudine said. They both laughed and closed their eyes at the same time. In unison they said: "1, 2, 3 and pointed to a color." Amazingly they both chose the color black. Claudine and Travis' eyes were huge. Smiles were bright. "You ready?" Travis asked. "Yes, I am." Claudine said. They grabbed each other's hand and proceeded into the "black" bathroom. This bathroom's shower was a thermostatic complete shower system with rough-in valve. On the wall of the shower were knobs to utilize dictating the pressure of the water coming out.   A hand-held shower wand could be used for bathing, or you could stand in front of the posts attached to the shower wall where if adjusted, water would flow from, and or you could stand under the shower head that was big enough to shower two adults standing under 6'5 (six feet 5 inches) tall.   The two of them took time to really look around in the luxurious bathroom.   Claudine walked over to the double sinks and starred in the mirror looking at Travis as he played with the water temperatures in the shower.   She then walked over to the black freestanding tub sitting close to the counter in the bathroom.

There was so much space in this bathroom. Travis said: "Babe, look. No way. There is even a closet in here with all black linen." Claudine rushed over to see. The hot water from the shower began to make the bathroom steamy. The mirrors fogged up quickly. They began to get undressed. Claudine walked over to the bathtub and grabbed one of the bath oils and foam bottles. She poured some of the foam inside the bathtub after stopping it up. She was getting the tub ready for the two of them. Besides it was over 6 feet long and deep. They looked at each other and then couldn't decide to bathe or shower together first.

"Toss a coin?" Travis said. They both laughed. Standing in the bathroom naked neither had a coin.

CHAPTER 3

I TABEMONO (GOOD FOOD)

A Japanese waitress walked up to the table where Travis and Claudine were sitting and said: (Hello. How may I help you?) "Kon'nichiwa watashi dono yo ni anata o tasukeru koto ga dekimasu ka." Travis just smiled and looked right into Claudine's eyes. He didn't have a clue as to what she was saying. The waitress giggled and whispered in English "Sorry, how may, I help you?" They all laughed. In Japanese Claudine responded: "Kon'nichiwa. Koko wa hajimetedesu." The waitress bowed her head and focused her attention more on Claudine. Travis sat back in awweee and smiled at his wife as she continued to order for them. On the ride there he pulled up the menu online and they discussed what each of them would like to try. With such appetites they wasted no time ordering. He was eager to surprise her with sightseeing. The waitress confirmed their orders. Looking at Travis first she said: "Anata ga motte iru Chahan." (You have-and she named the dish). He nodded in agreement. She then focused her attention on Claudine and said: "Anata ga motte iru Takikomi Gohan." (You have-and she named the dish.) Claudine nodded in agreement as well. She took their menus and said: "Modotte kimasu." (I'll be back). Claudine quickly said: "Watashiwa pinattsu areugi desu. (I have a peanut allergy.) The waitress said: "Hai." (Got it.) Claudine reached out to grab Travis' hand and he gently grabbed hers back. She smiled and said: "Although it doesn't come cheap, the experience of eating fucha ryori, Zen vegetarian dishes in Chinese manner, is an exquisite rarity. I am so glad I joined you. This is an amazing experience, and we are just getting started. So, have you decided to work remotely? Or are you still on the fence about it? It is training right, for now?" Claudine had a mouth full of questions. "My love I am so glad you joined me as well. I haven't decided just yet. I do want to make sure you are settled and somewhat more familiar with the basics around town before I choose. Part of me wants to experience training in their office. You know, get the Japanese experience. I know there will be translators available." (They both laughed). Travis got up from his side of the booth and sat beside Claudine. He whispered in her ear. "We didn't come this far for me to seem so far away. I still want to be the first face you see in the morning, touch throughout our days, and tuck each other in at night." She had such an amazing glow. Her smile was contagious. On lookers couldn't help but feel his words through her smile. Claudine whispered back: "Babe, always and forever." The two of them exchanged a kiss. Travis then lifted his head and said: "I've heard Kyoto-style tempura is light and delicate compared to the Tokyo variety. This (pointing to the table) Traditional inn-cum-restaurant serves some of the best in town, so I've heard and has a teahouse setting. That's what captured my attention. I'll see how I maneuver through this weekend and make my decision then." They shared a moment of silence and bright smiles. While they were waiting for their meals Travis grabbed Claudine's hand

and motioned for her to join him. He led the two of them to walk around. There were private rooms for evening kaiseki dinners overlooking a private classical garden. The atmosphere was great. They were there at the right time. The restaurant wasn't crowded. It had the right amount of people there to enjoy the scenery with. "I saw something online while we were back home. Something about a floating restaurant. I asked Karen at the office about it, you know she's a seafood lover. Well, her husband Rob is. He has traveled the world several times. She said he said to try Kanawa. That's the name of it. The restaurant. I'd love to try it." "Anything for you, my love." Travis said and kissed her hand. They hadn't reserved a private room but had walked into one and besides the temperature being perfect so was the view. No one was telling them they had to leave. The two of them found themselves sharing a bench looking at the garden. "I remember visiting my grandparents a lot when I was younger. It must have been summertime cause the heat was beating all of us up on the back of our necks. I tried to outrun it. But no matter how hard I tried I just couldn't. My cousin Sam was much faster and even he couldn't outrun the sun. Well, momma, that's what we called our grandma, she told us "ya'll can go outside. Even to the courts. But whatever you do don't go walking across Mr. Paul's grass. He gets it cut just the way he likes it, and I don't wanna hear that old man fussing today bout no footprints. He always says the only footprints he needs to see are Jesus' when he is carrying him. Hea me?" We'd respond: "Yes, momma." And we'd dash out of the door before she had a chance to ask us to do chores or changed her mind about us playing. She knew we'd end up back in the house soon. Sam had a thing for walking on Mr. Paul's grass and hearing him fuss." Claudine giggled. "Well, this particular day Mr. Paul didn't yell out of his kitchen window, dash out of his door, he didn't respond to Sam trampling on his grass at all. We were confused but we didn't continue to make noise. We went on about our business and headed to the courts as usual. Boy was it hot. By the time we were closer to meeting up with our friends Sam suggested we go to Ms. Brenda's house, she was the candy lady. She had all the goodies. They were cheap too. (Claudine giggled again). We got in her house and grabbed so much stuff you would have thought we went grocery shopping. (They both laughed.) Crazy thing though, as we got closer to meeting up with our friends it's like the weather and the air was changing right before our eyes. None of the fellas were rushing up to us to grab the snacks. They usually wouldn't let us get that close without grabbing and snatching something. Nope. Not that day. They were sitting around faces full of gloom and energy depleted. So, I asked "what's all the long faces for?" No one wanted to be the first to answer. Sam said: "Dang, ya'll acting like ya'll lost ya best friend or something." We all looked at one another counting the faces. Everyone was present. I shrugged my shoulders. Then as soon as I said: "Anybody heard from Mr. Paul?" The air got so thick I felt sick to my stomach without even knowing what had happened. "Yeah, Lucy said he had a stroke the other day while we were in school. She said if he doesn't get any better, she and her momma gone have to move again. They ain't got no place to go. We sat there in silence for what seemed like an hour. It was just a few seconds. Lucky spoke up and asked: "So, now what? Can we go see him or something?" No one said a word. We didn't feel like playing basketball that day or playing nothing else. We just kinda sat around, ate our snacks, drank our sodas, and chilled. No one was in

the mood for fun. A few hours had passed,
and we found ourselves sharing all the "Mr.
Paul" stories. He'd tell us so many about
when he was growing up. The one that
stuck out the most was him using his
imagination about traveling. He'd pull
pages out of magazines and make believe he
visited some of the most beautiful places in
the world. None of us knew at first but Mr.
Paul was adopted. Other than being in the
system and so many different houses all his
life he'd never traveled before. That's kinda
why I am the way I am. Well, the traveling
part of me. Cause of Mr. Paul. He lived his
entire life and up until that point had never

been anywhere outside of where he was born. I promised myself I'd travel as often as I could and to everywhere if the good Lord allowed me to." Travis was all man, yet he was a sensitive man. Memories and him talking about Mr. Paul caused his eyes to become misty. He cleared his throat a few times and held Claudine's hand a little tighter. His throat had a knot in it but he managed to get himself together just in time for the waitress to make her way over to them. "Sumimasen." (Excuse me.) The waitress said. They both looked up to her. She then said: "Anata no shokuji wa junbi ga dekite imasu." (Your meal is ready.)

Travis and Claudine both said in unison: "Arigatogzaimashita." (Thank you.) Claudine and the waitress both were impressed. Travis hadn't shared with Claudine that he knew any words in Japanese. The waitress even bowed her head and gave him a brighter smile. It was as if she were proud of him too. Travis smiled back and as he and Claudine stood up, he stepped behind her as she followed the waitress to their table. Whispering and looking back at him Claudine said: "Good job babe. I wonder what other words you know. Let's practice later tonight." She winked at him. Travis popped her rear end

and said: "Thank you. Ok!"